CW00859775

Magical Mia

Super Self-Talk!

Julie Cassetta

Elena Taranenko

"The way we talk to our children becomes their inner voice"

Peggy O'Mara

To my parents — for nurturing my positive inner voice and for always believing in me and encouraging all my many dreams.

Published by Grow Good Publishing
Copyright © 2021 Grow Good Publishing

For information contact:
Julie Cassetta at www.juliecassetta.com
Written by: Julie Cassetta
Illustrated by: Elena Taranenko
ISBN: 978-1-7364208-3-6 (Hardback)
ISBN: 978-1-7364208-4-3 (paperback)
Library of Congress Control Number: 2021922048
Printed in the United States of America
10 9 8 7 6 5 4 3 2 1
First Edition: November 2021

On a MAGICAL Saturday — such a nice day,
all my friends at the park called me over to play.

They were all playing soccer which I'd never tried.
But it looked like such fun and I LOVE it outside!

I said, "Hi Sam and Jada! Hello Ben and Kay!
I'm so glad we're all here on this excellent day!"

I was there with my friends and felt happy inside.
We all started to sparkle. Our smiles growing wide!

When I'm playing with friends, I see magic **expand**,
because friendship grows magic, they go hand-in-hand.
Jada said, "Be on my team and just kick toward the goal.
Stop the other team stealing the ball for control."

Then, we started to play, and I missed every shot!
I was tired and frustrated, sweaty, and hot.

I kept fumbling the ball. I was **always** behind.
I was awkward and slow, but my friends didn't mind.
Soon my energy vanished and so did my glow.
As my sparkle stopped sparkling, I felt really low.

I said, "I'm bad at soccer. You're better than me."
Sam said, "We've played all year, and you're new. Can't you see?
So, let's go take a break. I can see you're upset.
You have made a great start. You'll get better, I bet!"

I replied, "I'm no good – can't do ANYTHING right.
I'm the worst there can be. You're just being polite."

"If you quit now,"
said Jada, "you won't get to see
how much fun you could have
and how good you can be."

"We'd all miss you, of course;
it would not be the same.
We can all play together
and teach you the game!"

Kay said, "This may sound strange,
but there's something I do.
It's a trick that I use which might also help you."

"There are times I pretend that two parrots are speaking.
With one on each shoulder, the good one, I'm seeking."

"The bad parrot says what is mean and untrue,
making everything worse — 'til I'm feeling quite blue.

But the good parrot always will be on my side.
And it says I'll accomplish things once I have tried.
It reminds me I'm **perfect** – created just right.
When I hear those good thoughts, I feel joy and delight."

You're perfect the way you are!

I said, "Look, my bad parrot will never be quiet. It's **squawking** so loudly, it's hard to deny it."

Kay answered, "I know when my bad parrot's leading. I send it AWAY, so it won't be succeeding."

"That's funny!" I said. "I'll start thinking that way.
I can see my bad parrot has too much to say!"

"When I have nasty thoughts that are filling my head,
I won't listen; I'll choose my good parrot instead."

I said "Let's all keep playing. I'll stop feeling blue."
They all answered, "You've got this! You know we LOVE YOU!"

I could feel magic grow from their kind and sweet words.
I was feeling their magic – **not hearing that bird!**

I would try to have fun and not care how I played.
And I got a lot better because I had stayed.
I'm so proud I stuck with it and didn't go home.
I was there with my teammates — not sad and alone.

I was **growing** my magic. My friends helped me see,
by directing my thoughts, I can choose who to be.

So, the next time you miss when you try something new,

that's completely okay! You're just PERFECTLY YOU!

NEGATIVE THOUGHTS
THAT MAKE YOU FEEL BAD

What's the use?

Everyone is better than me.

What if everyone laughs at me?

I can't do anything right.

I quit.

This is going to be awful.

No one understands me.

Why is everything so hard?

I'm horrible.

I shouldn't have made that mistake.

I'll never get this.

Nothing ever goes right.

Why do bad things always happen to me?

It's all my fault.

WHAT YOU CAN CHOOSE
TO THINK INSTEAD

I can do hard things!

If my friend said this
about themself,
what would I tell them?

Is this thought
helping me?

Is there someone I
can ask for help?

Is what I'm thinking
really true?

I can choose how
I respond!

I'll keep trying.

I'm perfect the
way I am.

Mistakes are how
I learn.

I'm great at a
lot of things!

My brain grows when
I try new things.

I know I'll get better if I
keep trying and don't quit.

My life is beautiful.

What would the people
that care about me say?

CPSIA information can be obtained
at www.ICGtesting.com
Printed in the USA
LVHW072101161121
703499LV00007B/286

* 9 7 8 1 7 3 6 4 2 0 8 3 6 *